Kinsey's KIDNEY Adventure

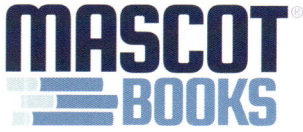

www.mascotbooks.com

Kinsey's Kidney Adventure

©2017 LiveOnNY Foundation. All Rights Reserved. No part of this publication may be reproduced, stored in a retrieval system or transmitted in any form by any means electronic, mechanical, or photocopying, recording or otherwise without the permission of the author.

For more information, please contact:
Mascot Books
560 Herndon Parkway #120
Herndon, VA 20170
info@mascotbooks.com

Library of Congress Control Number: 2017905350

CPSIA Code: PBANG0517A
ISBN-13: 978-1-68401-376-0

Printed in the United States

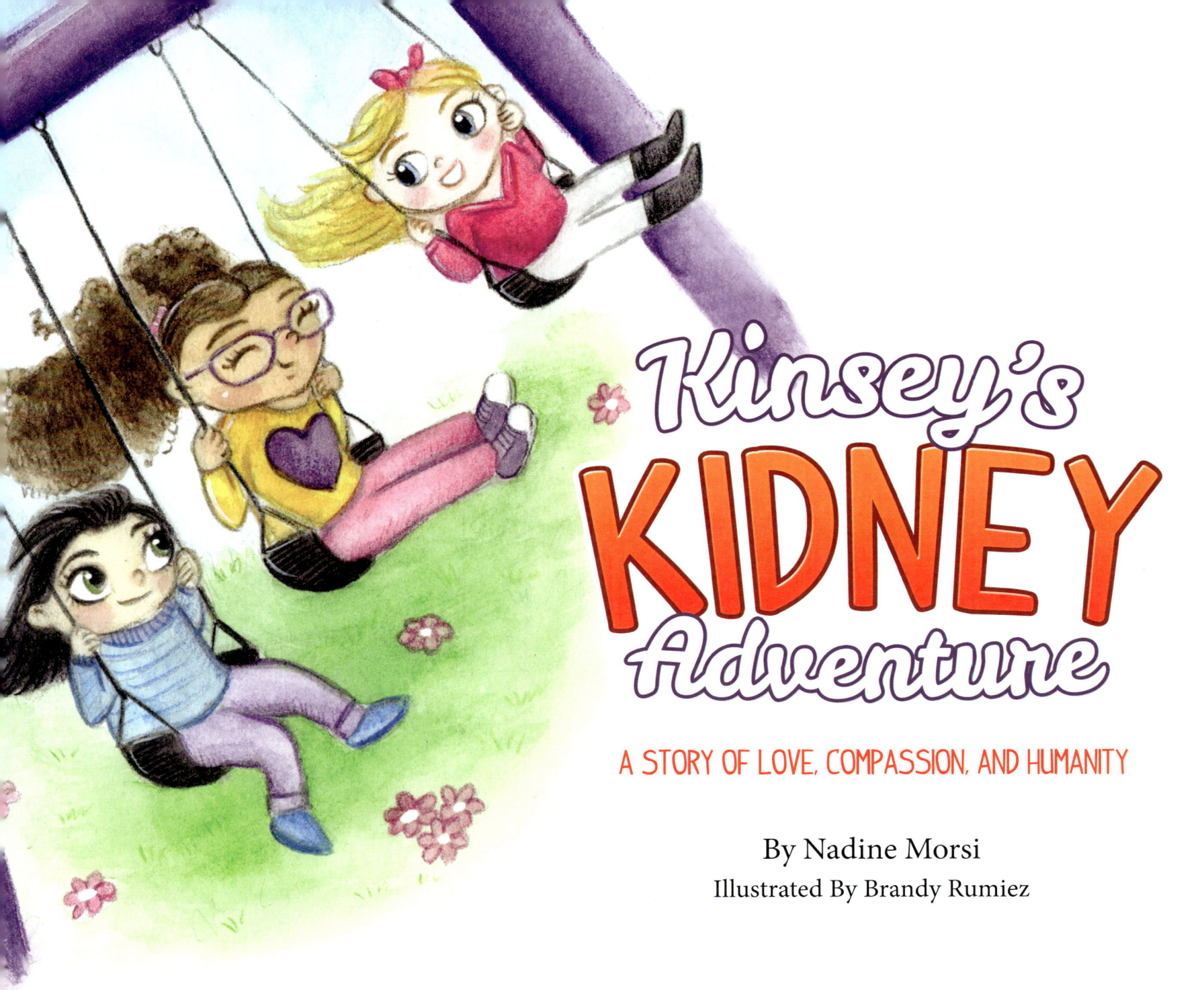

Kinsey's KIDNEY Adventure

A STORY OF LOVE, COMPASSION, AND HUMANITY

By Nadine Morsi

Illustrated By Brandy Rumiez

Dedication

For Kinsey, my beautiful, brave, resilient daughter –
the inspiration and motivation behind everything I do.
For Kinsey's hero, her anonymous donor.
For Galal Morsi, my beloved late father, a liver
recipient and our guardian angel.

Hi, my name is Kinsey, and I'm in a kindergarten class.
I may be just five, but I've got lots of spunk and sass.

I love going to the park with my friends to play.
Laughing, singing, and cooking with Mom often fills my day.

For a few months I've been feeling very tired, weak, and sick.
My appetite is not so good, I feel like I'm carrying a heavy brick.

I was having frequent stomach aches and even throwing up – YUCK!
Staying home and missing school and fun play dates was just my luck!

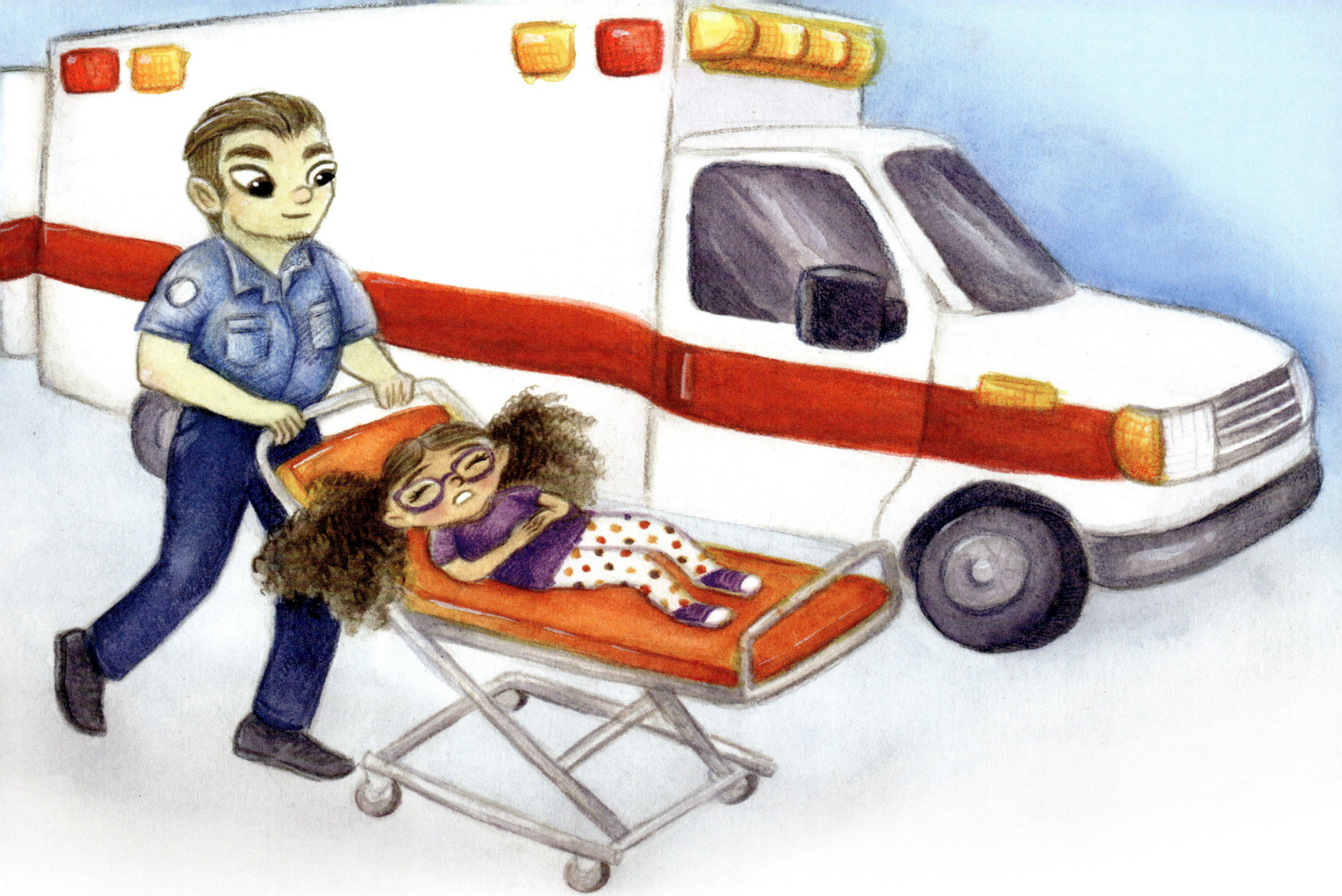

I wasn't feeling any better and was rushed to the emergency room.
And just like that my life turned upside down –
KABOOM!

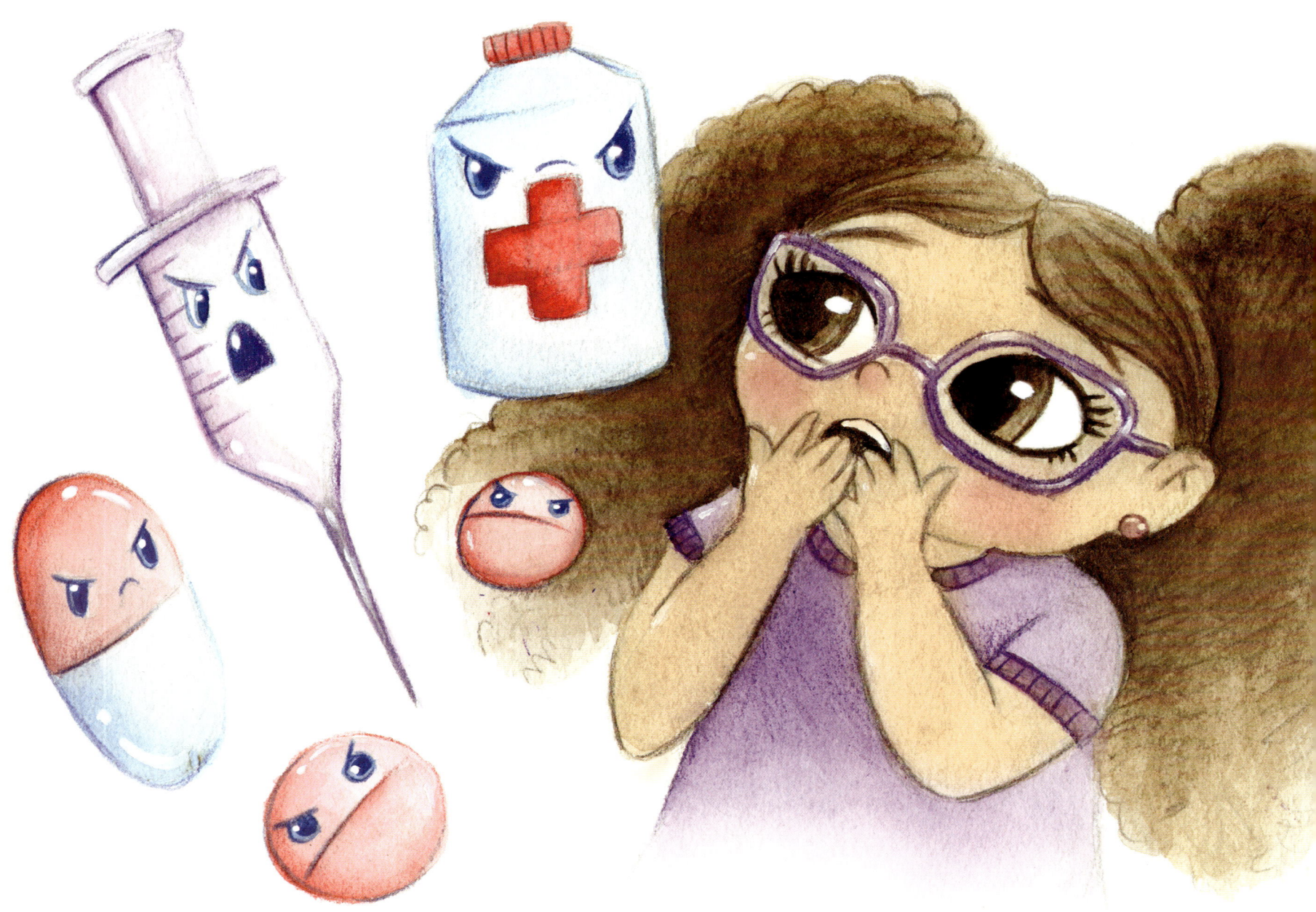

Hospitals are sometimes a scary place to be.
Doctors, nurses, medications, and the dreaded IV.

I had to overcome my fears and be very brave.
Listen to the doctors, for my life they had to save.

Some of the tests did hurt a little – OUCH!
All I wanted was to go home and curl up on my couch.

The doctors told my mommy my kidneys weren't working right.
And I would have to be super strong to overcome this fight.

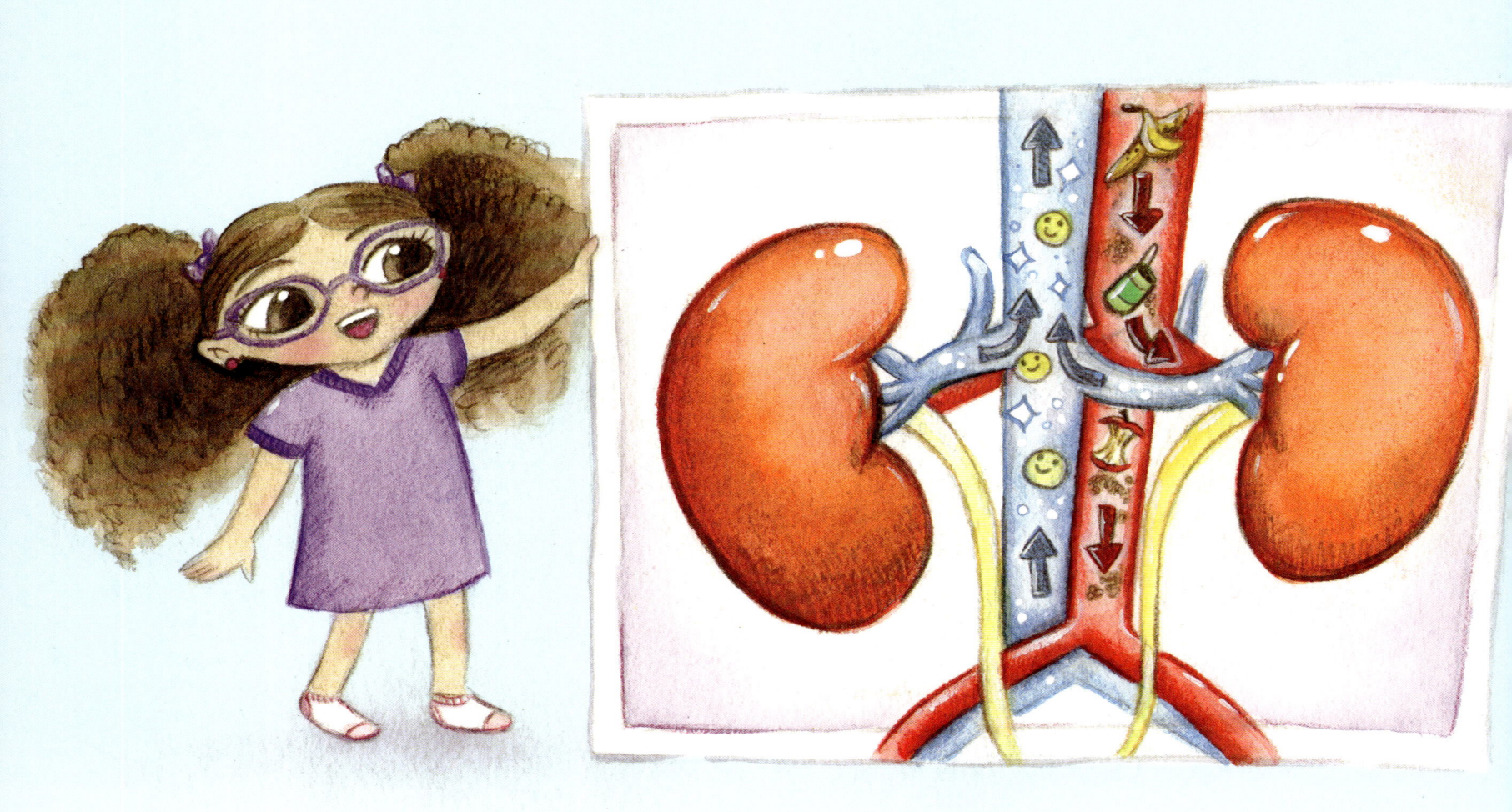

Your kidneys are two bean shaped organs that help you survive.
They clean your blood and remove fluid to help keep you alive.

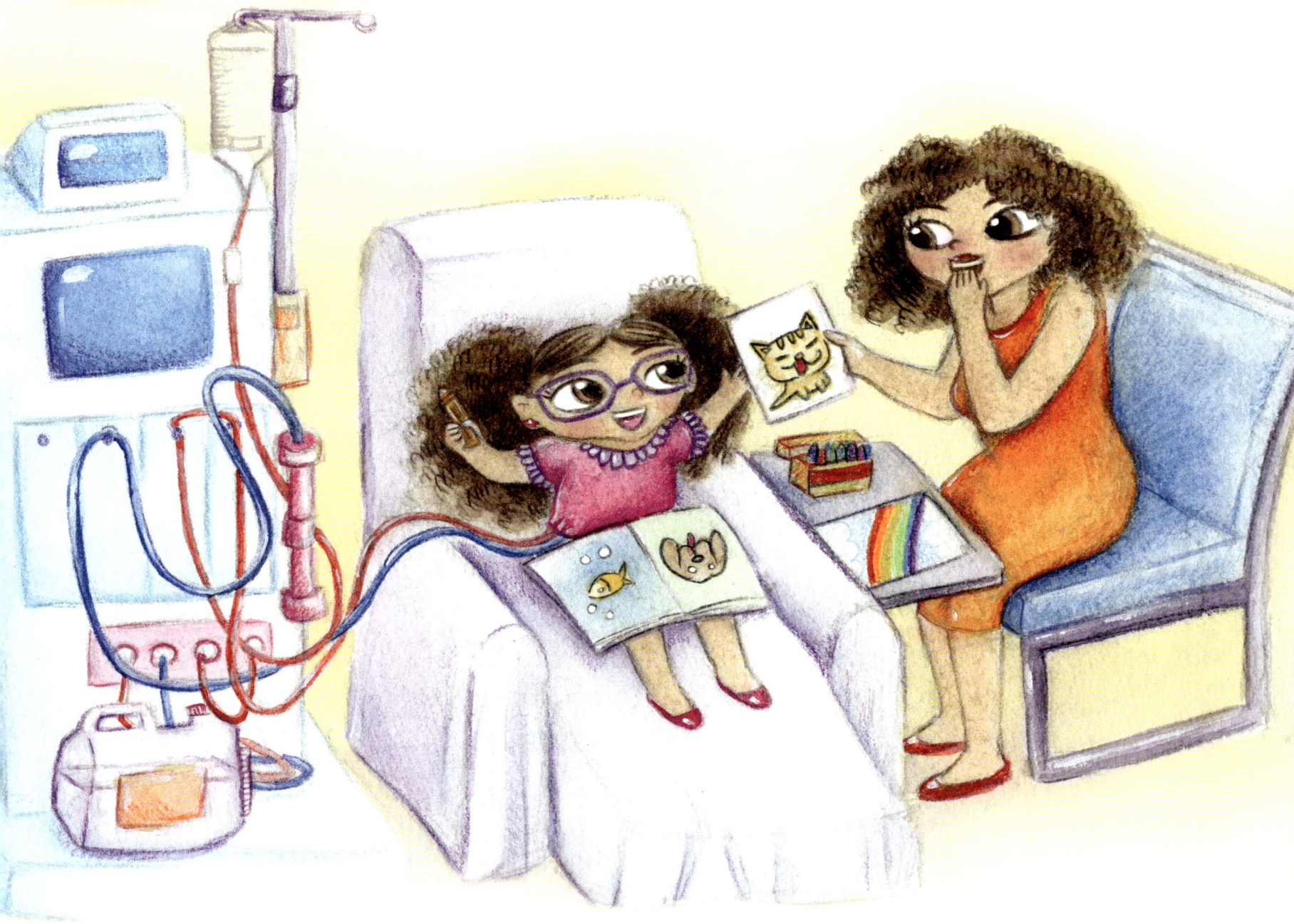

Dialysis is a machine I was put on to help my kidneys do their job.
Some days I would be happy, some days I would sob.

At times, I felt sad about the bananas, pizza, and ice cream I could no longer eat,
But thankfully, I could still have my favorite – strawberries, *oh so sweet!*

While I was receiving treatment at the hospital and connected to the machine,
I met the sweetest, most caring and loving nurses any one had ever seen!

Many people came flooding into my life who were incredible and kind.
Wanting to help in every way, hoping a solution they would find.

The best solution was surgery and finding a new kidney for me.
So I'd no longer be attached to a machine, and live a life where I was free.

I wasn't so sure what a kidney transplant would entail.
But, I felt in my heart, it was a task I would not fail.

A kidney donor hero was finally found and on his way.
To help me return to living the life I had and save the day.

A complete stranger decided to give one of his kidneys to me.
We are all born with two, but you can share one, you see!

And so with strength, hope, and courage, back to the hospital I went.
Knowing this was something I had to do to live the life I've always dreamt.

The morning of the surgery, my donor and I walked in hand in hand.
Smiling, I found the courage and strength, though this wasn't what I planned.

I must admit that during this time, I felt a bit worried and scared.
What got me through those feelings was knowing so many people cared.

The doctor gave me some funny feeling medicine to make me go to sleep.
And just like that, I was out like a light – not a sound, not a peep.

Not a thing did I feel during surgery as my sleep was very deep.
When I woke up I had a new kidney – one that was mine, one I could keep!

My mommy's face was looking down at me, beaming with so much pride.
She was happy I was feeling better, never once leaving my side.

I was taken to a special floor where new people I would meet.
One of whom was a boy named Ryan, who was pretty cool and neat.

Ryan also received a new organ like me, but his was a heart.
And he was just as eager as I was to have a brand new start.

You will be surprised how much strength you have when facing a hard time.
The mountain may be high and hilly, but it's one you can surely climb.

My story made it to the *Daily News* for everyone in the whole wide world to see –YIPPEE!
And through a donor chain, another hero named Jannie saved twelve more people just like me!

A donor chain is when a person decides to share one of his kidneys with another
to selflessly save the life of a friend, child, mother, father, sister, or brother!

Ryan and I are both grateful to our donors for the decision they made.
We will always remember them in our lives for the awesome role they played.

Off to having fun play dates and eating my favorite foods I go.
To racing to the park and frolicking in the snow!

To returning to school and dance class, and traveling with my mom.
To breathing better, running faster, and feeling peaceful and calm.

My life is a little different now, there are medications I must take.
It's not so bad, I promise you, especially with yummy cake!

Before I go, I'd like you to know how special people are.
Some are with us here, and some shine down upon us like a star.

Their presence is forever felt for a part of them they leave.
They fill our hearts with promise and light, and make us all believe.

This journey that I went on had its ups and downs, it's true!
But I made it to the finish line and my life began anew!

So, if you ever go through something hard and "I can't make it" is what you think.
Just close your eyes, take a deep breath, and it will be over in a blink.

Sometimes in life you must face things that you fear.
You are not alone, you are loved, and everyone will cheer!

You may not know all the answers, especially when you ask yourself "Why?"
Just promise me you will push through your challenge and give it your best try!

Acknowledgments

First and foremost, I would like to thank Kinsey's humble and incredibly kind anonymous donor, who selflessly, with conviction and no hesitation, put her needs before his own. You are the reason she gets to continue to enjoy her life and share her story. Our love and gratitude will always live on for you.

Many thanks to all of my friends and family for believing in me, Kinsey, and this project. I would like to also give special thanks to our Facebook army of supporters who tirelessly shared her story, never gave up hope, devoted their free time and late nights, and fought hard alongside us. Your prayers, strength, and support helped us make it to the "finish line."

Very special thanks and gratitude goes out to:

Helen Irving, CEO and President of LiveOnNY, for her enthusiastic support from the moment I brought the book idea to her.

Heidi Evans, a brilliant and dedicated writer and journalist, who first shared our story in the *New York Daily News* and has been instrumental in bringing the book to life at the LiveOnNY Foundation. Thank you, too, for your creative ideas and guidance.

The LiveOnNY Foundation for generously funding this project through contributions from Donate Eight, Lap4Life, the Marcie Mazzola Foundation, and the John Acquaro North Shore Bike Ride for Organ Donation Awareness.

Brandy Rumiez, artist extraordinaire, who so perfectly captured Kinsey's story through her beautiful illustrations.

Kinsey's team of medical professionals, including her wonderful nephrologists and nurses at Cohen Children's Medical Center in New Hyde Park for their outstanding care and compassion that continues to this day. The transplant medical team at The Mount Sinai Hospital in Manhattan, including her amazing transplant surgeon, Dr. Scott Ames, and the team of incredible nephrologists for their unparalleled level of care.

Children throughout NYC public schools and their families, including Kinsey's elementary school, PS 188Q, for organizing walks and fundraisers, sending cards and beautiful artwork that brightened Kinsey's hospital and dialysis days.

All donors, both living and deceased, for teaching us invaluable lessons on humanity, compassion, and sacrifice.

And to the staff at Mascot Books who edited, published, and marketed the book with enthusiasm.

Finally, I would like to thank my sweet, little girl, Kinsey who showed such resilience, courage, and strength while flashing her bright smile throughout her journey. In her nine years on Earth, she has taught me more about life than I have ever known. I can't wait to learn even more lessons from you and watch you grow into a remarkable young woman.

For more information about organ donation and/or how to register to become a life saver, please visit:

www.donatelifeamerica.org

www.liveonny.org

www.unos.org

www.organdonor.gov

About the Author

Nadine Morsi is a licensed pediatric Occupational Therapist with 17 years of experience working with children with special needs for the New York City Department of Education. She received her Master's Degree in Occupational Therapy from Columbia University. She is a tireless advocate for the cause of organ donation, and lives in New York City with her sassy and spunky nine-year-old daughter, Kinsey.

About the Illustrator

Brandy Rumiez is a professional illustrator, painter, and sculptor who puts her heart into her art and everything she does. Her work has been exhibited locally and nationally and has been recognized for its bright energetic colors, subtle humor, and whimsy. She is based in South Florida. To view her portfolio, visit brumiez.com.

Van Stolatis Photography
van@vanstolatisphotography.com

About Kinsey

Kinsey is a happy and healthy 4th grader. She loves to dance, play basketball, do arts and crafts, and play with her friends and cousins, Zach and Evan. She would like to be a kidney doctor and a pastry chef when she grows up.

Tips for discussing organ donation with your child/student:

The topic of organ donation is one that can be difficult for children to conceptualize or understand and just as difficult for parents/educators to feel comfortable approaching with them. In order to alleviate any anxiety or fear that children can experience when approaching the topic, here are some tips to keep in mind:

- Reassure them that not every child who gets ill will ever need an organ and that this only affects a certain very small population of children.
- Reassure them that they are healthy and that all of their organs are working well and doing the job that they were made to do.
- Remind them that the book was written to increase their compassion for children who have a serious illness—to show them how brave and strong they can be as well as showing the values of kindness, sharing, and empathy.

The following are answers to some common questions I have encountered when reading the book to school age children.

1. Why did Kinsey get sick? Can I get sick like her?

Kinsey's kidneys were not working well which made her very sick and tired all the time. Your kidneys are very strong and working just fine. In fact, it is very unlikely that you will get sick like her. There are some children that are born with a particular condition that makes them more likely to develop kidney disease. Kinsey's specific condition is extremely rare.

2. Why didn't Kinsey's Mom share her kidney with Kinsey?

In order to qualify to be a living donor, one has to not only be a match but also be in excellent health. Although Kinsey's Mom was a match for Kinsey, she was unable to donate her kidney because of an existing medical condition of her own. Donors are very carefully screened and must go through a series of tests before they can qualify to be donors.

3. What happened to the person who gave Kinsey his kidney?

Kinsey's donor is doing very well and is perfectly healthy. Remember, you have two kidneys and you only need one good healthy kidney in order to live. Kinsey's donor decided that he wanted to share one of his kidneys with her to make her feel better.

4. What happened to the person who gave his heart to Ryan?

There are some organs that you cannot share while you are still living. For example, you only have one heart. Ryan's donor passed away before giving her organ to Ryan. A donor makes the decision to donate his/her healthy organs before they die. Their wish is to help others in need when they can no longer use their organs for their own body anymore. Even though they passed away from an accident or an illness beyond their control, their organs can continue to live on in others and make very sick people feel well again.

5. Did the surgery hurt Kinsey? How did it feel?

Kinsey did not feel anything throughout her surgery. She was given some medicine to make her go to sleep. When she woke up from the surgery, she was given medication to make her feel better and more comfortable. Kinsey felt a little bit nervous and scared before the surgery, but she was very brave and knew that this was something she had to do in order to live, feel better, and return to her normal activities.

Tips continued:

6. Can I be an organ donor too?
In almost every state in the country, you can sign up to be an organ donor when you are sixteen years old. Many young people sign up when they apply for their learner's permit or driver's license. It's also a good idea to discuss this with your parents so they know your wishes.

7. What is an organ donor chain?
A donor chain begins when a person, like Jannie, decides to donate their kidney out of the goodness of their heart to someone else that needs a kidney and is a good match. Then, a family member or friend of the person who received Jannie's kidney donates one of their kidneys to another stranger who is also a good match and so on and so on. A special computer program matches donors and recipients across the country. One of the longest kidney donor chains so far has involved sixty people!

Classroom/Parent Discussion Questions:

- Is this a real or imaginary story?
- How are you and Kinsey similar/different?
- What character traits does Kinsey possess?
- What character traits does Kinsey's donor possess? Why do you think Kinsey's donor decided to share one of his kidneys with her?
- Kinsey's donor was able to share a piece of him with her. Can you remember a time where you shared something special with someone else? How did that make you feel?
- What is the message of this story? What is the author trying to convey to the reader?
- How do you think Kinsey felt when she went through this experience? Sequence the events in the story and discuss some of the emotions she may have been feeling from the beginning to the end of her journey.
- As a child, how can I help children who may be sick like Kinsey?
- As an adult, what can I do to help other people like Kinsey?
- How did people come together to help Kinsey in her time of need? Can you think of a time in your life where your friend or family member needed your help? What did you do to help them?
- How did Kinsey get through her difficult time?
- What does the author mean by "some are with us here, and some shine down upon us like a star"?
- What did receiving a transplant mean for Kinsey? How has her life changed since the transplant?
- Can you name some organs in your body and what their functions are?